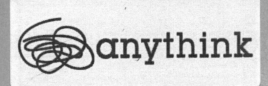

For my magical friends, Steph and Mary,
who make the world a more sparkly place. –K.D.

To each of our own unique differences.
After all, they make up what's interesting about our world. –R.F.

Katherine Tegen Books is an imprint of HarperCollins Publishers.

Oona and the Shark
Text copyright © 2022 by Kelly DiPucchio
Illustrations copyright © 2022 by Raissa Figueroa
All rights reserved. Manufactured in Italy.

Library of Congress Cataloging-in-Publication Data
Names: DiPucchio, Kelly, author. | Figueroa, Raissa, illustrator.
Title: Oona and the shark / words by Kelly DiPucchio ; pictures by Raissa Figueroa.
Description: First edition. | New York : Katherine Tegen Books, [2022] | Audience: Ages 4-8. | Audience: Grades K-1. |
    Summary: Oona the mermaid is friends with everyone, but when her attempts to befriend a shark with sensory
    issues fail miserably, she realizes what may be fun for her may be overwhelming for him.
Identifiers: LCCN 2020047039 | ISBN 978-0-06-307142-1 (hardcover)
Subjects: CYAC: Sensory disorders—Fiction. | Mermaids—Fiction. | Sharks—Fiction. | Friendship—Fiction.
Classification: LCC PZ7.D6219 Oo 2022 | DDC [E]—dc23
LC record available at https://lccn.loc.gov/2020047039

The artist used Procreate to create the digital illustrations for this book.
Typography and lettering by Molly Fehr
21 22 23 24 25   RTLO   10 9 8 7 6 5 4 3 2 1

❖

First Edition

Oona
and the Shark

words by
Kelly DiPucchio

pictures by
Raissa Figueroa

KATHERINE TEGEN BOOKS
An Imprint of HarperCollins Publishers

Like most mermaids, Oona
was good at making friends.

Otto was her friend.

The **pelicans** were her friends.

Even the *hermit crabs* (who weren't exactly friendly) were her friends.

So when Oona met Stanley, she hoped **he** would be her friend too.

She insisted on sharing some of her favorite treasures with the shark.
But Stanley was particular.

He didn't care for the **hat**

or the **horn**.

And definitely
not the **squeaky,**
squeaky
unicorn!

Oona was an inventor, and like most inventors, she was eager to show off her latest creations to her friends.

The Beach Ball Juggler.

The Sandcastle Maker.

The Seahorse Carousel.

But Stanley was too busy with his seashell collection to pay her any mind.

That just confused Oona and made her *more* determined to impress the shark.

So, she built **new** inventions.

Bigger.

Bolder.

LOUDER INVENTIONS!

Oona built inventions that **hopped!**

Inventions that **chopped!**

And inventions that . . .

ED!

But all that noisy *hopping* and *chopping* and *popping* just made Stanley **ANGRY**.

By and large, mermaids are stubborn, and Oona was no exception. So what she did next was *exactly* what any other mermaid would have done under the circumstances.

She threw a party. *Who doesn't love a party?*

Stanley! That's who doesn't love a party!

Understandably, Oona's feelings were *hurt*. But Oona knew (as mermaids do) that she was magical, and if Stanley didn't want to be her friend . . .

she would still be magical.

Oona dove off her rock and swam to the bottom of the ocean floor. It was peaceful and quiet down there with the jellyfish and the sea turtles.

It was peaceful and quiet! YES! OF COURSE!

Why hadn't she figured it out sooner?
The horn! The inventions! The party! *Stanley didn't like noise.*
Or distractions.
Or crowded bouncy castles.

Something twinkled in the sand,
catching Oona's eye.
Sea glass! It gave her an idea.

Oona returned to her workshop.
She drew up plans with Otto.

She took measurements with the eels.

And she gathered tools and supplies
from her land friends.

By the light of the lantern fish,
Oona worked late into the night.

The Hydropower Super Sea Glass Sorter was whisper quiet and it was

MAGNIFICENT.

Oona set up her brand-new invention near Stanley's cove and, without saying a word, she began feeding the machine.

Each piece of sea glass she sent down the conveyor belt tumbled through a series of long tubes and curvy chutes before dropping into the correct jar.

Blue.
Blue.

White.
White.

Green.
Green.

The curious shark watched from a safe distance.
Blue. White. Green.

Stanley swam a little closer
to get a better look.
Blue. White. Green.

Soon the shark who had been so hard to reach was by Oona's side.

"Would you like to help?" Oona asked Stanley.
Stanley nodded.
Blue. White. Green.
Oona smiled.
Stanley smiled back.

The two of them played side by side.
They were quiet . . .
together.

And together they had **FUN**.